Mrs. Hrehocik,

I am so glad you enjoyed reading our book. Illustrating this story took a long time but it was a great experience. I hope that your future classes of students can enjoy it as much as I did. Thank you for sharing our story of Rosey!

♡ Sarena Chirdon ♡

MW00763605

Rosey
Makes
Sense

By Melissa Israel

Illustrated by
Sarena Chirdon

This book is dedicated to my husband Pete
and 3 children, Grant, Kennedy and Delaney...
Together, we make sense!

Near the edge of a wondrous forest, many animals reside.
They move through the night and they scurry in stride.

Looking for dinner to fill big appetites,
Chasing their hunger through each star-filled night.

As sunshine warms each afternoon, some animals
simply sleep...
While neighborhoods awaken with much business
to keep.

But Rosey the Skunk's thoughts seemed to
jumpstart her heart.
Sleeping was a challenge from the moment
she'd start.

Her wakeful moments filled up with dreams,
For life as a skunk was a challenge it seems.

Rosey would scurry through the night in her prowl,
Getting thunderous attention from each dog
that would howl.

Her presence was never welcomed from anyone
she'd see...
For when she was spotted, all quickly seemed to flee!

Squirrels would go soaring to
the highest treetops,
Bunnies would burrow without pausing to stop.

Rosey did not like how this all made her feel;
She wished that her talents had
a grander appeal.

Rosey wanted a lifestyle that lived up to her name.
But cries to her mother reflected more shame.

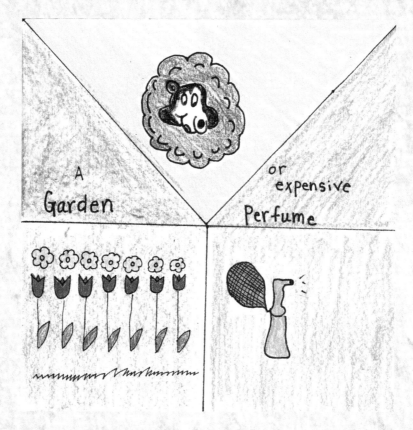

She'd dreamed of fresh flowers like a garden
in bloom...
She wished to be sought after like
expensive perfume.

Rosey's visions captured a more pleasant smell...
And this showed in the stories, sweet Rosey
would tell.

"Oh Mommy how I wish that my scent was
more sweet"...
"Like the aroma of cookies baked fresh
as a treat!"

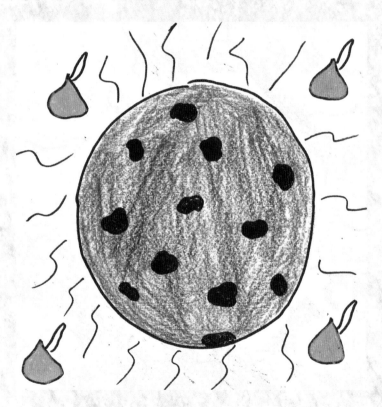

"The hint of sweet chocolate to fill up the air"...
Her mom shook her head while weighed
in despair.

"I see how clean linens blow in the breeze...
How their freshness spills from them with the greatest
of ease!"

"Oh Rosey, my daughter, with such big dreams to tell...
A flower? A cookie? Or linens to smell?"

"These things are all lovely, but could never
be YOU...
For you were made to be skunk-like, this I know
to be true."

"Cookies are eaten and flowers are picked..."
"Linens stretched across mattresses sometimes
too thick!"

"But you have something special that helps
you to live...
Danger can't lurk closely with the scent
you can give!"

"To hear of your wishes to be different
and new...
Makes me sad since I want you to
LIKE BEING YOU!"

"You share such great talents in the stories
you spin...
But I want you to be thankful standing in
your own skin!"

Her attempts to gain clarity came without
a surprise,
Her mother was loving, patient and wise.

With wisdom to ponder, Rosey went off to rest,
It was hard to relax with so much on her chest.

As thoughts bounced and collided in her worrying
mind,
She heard a desperate squeak, sneak up
from behind...

Spotting two chipmunks ready to race...
Beneath a drooling cat with satisfaction
on his face...

Danger can not lurk closely with the scent you can give...

Feeling the stir of building suspense,
Rosey's mom's words echoed and it all made more
sense...

Sneaking out quickly from her quiet resting spot,
Rosey knew she was needed - she'd have only ONE
shot!

Curling up her belly, her tail toward the sky,
Puffing out a scent that would water most eyes.

The feline stood troubled, with his head
in the cloud,
A scent far from "rosey", but for once
she was proud!

Cat hobbled away without looking back,
Two grateful chipmunks would not be
cat's snack.

In a moment of sweetness, Rosey lived up
to her name...
Making *scents* of her life, would bring
her some fame.

A hero that night, with victory and glory...
Rosey's life would continue like the sweetest
of stories!

Made in the USA
Lexington, KY
12 February 2014